Dear Parent:
Your child's love of reading starts here!

Every child learns to read in a different way and at his or her own speed. Some go back and forth between reading levels and read favorite books again and again. Others read through each level in order. You can help your young reader improve and become more confident by encouraging his or her own interests and abilities. From books your child reads with you to the first books he or she reads alone, there are I Can Read Books for every stage of reading:

SHARED READING
Basic language, word repetition, and whimsical illustrations, ideal for sharing with your emergent reader

BEGINNING READING
Short sentences, familiar words, and simple concepts for children eager to read on their own

READING WITH HELP
Engaging stories, longer sentences, and language play for developing readers

READING ALONE
Complex plots, challenging vocabulary, and high-interest topics for the independent reader

ADVANCED READING
Short paragraphs, chapters, and exciting themes for the perfect bridge to chapter books

I Can Read Books have introduced children to the joy of reading since 1957. Featuring award-winning authors and illustrators and a fabulous cast of beloved characters, I Can Read Books set the standard for beginning readers.

A lifetime of discovery begins with the magical words **"I Can Read!"**

Visit www.icanread.com for information on enriching your child's reading experience.

For stargazers everywhere
—J.O'C.

For Yarden and Yonatan,
who shine brightly in my heart
—R.P.G.

For the PA Stargazers,
whose friendship bends the Space/Time Continuum
—T.E.

www.icanread.com

Library of Congress Cataloging-in-Publication Data
O'Connor, Jane.
Fancy Nancy sees stars / by Jane O'Connor ; cover illustration by Robin Preiss Glasser ; interior illustrations by Ted Enik. — 1st ed.
p. cm. — (I can read book) (Fancy Nancy)
Summary: When a rainstorm prevents Nancy and her friend Robert from getting to the planetarium the night of a class field trip, she has a brilliant idea for making things better.
ISBN 978-0-06-123611-2 (pbk.) — ISBN 978-0-06-123612-9 (trade bdg.)
[1. Astronomy—Fiction. 2. School field trips—Fiction. 3. Planetariums—Fiction.] I. Enik, Ted, ill. II. Title.
PZ7.O222Fgs 2009 2008010284
[E]—dc22 CIP
AC

10 11 12 13 14 LP/WOR 10 9 ❖ First Edition

by Jane O'Connor

cover illustration by Robin Preiss Glasser

interior illustrations by Ted Enik

HarperCollins*Publishers*

Stars are so fascinating.
(That's a fancy word
for interesting.)
I love how they sparkle in the sky.

Tonight is our class trip.

Yes! It’s a class trip at night!

We are going to the planetarium.

That is a museum

about stars and planets.

Ms. Glass tells us,

“The show starts at eight.

We will all meet there.”

I smile at my friend Robert.

My parents are taking Robert and me.

Then Ms. Glass asks,

“What star is closest to Earth?”

That’s easy.

It’s the sun.

"What do you call stars
that make a picture?"
asks Ms. Glass.
Robert and Bree have both forgotten.
"I know, I know," I say.
"A constellation."

Ms. Glass nods.

On the wall are pictures.

There's the hunter and the crab

and the Big Dipper.

It looks like a big spoon.

We will see all of them at the show.

I can hardly wait.

At home, Robert and I
put glow-in-the-dark stickers
on our T-shirts.
Mine has the Big Dipper.
Robert has the hunter on his.

We spin my mobile

and watch the planets orbit the sun.

(Orbit is a fancy word.

It means to travel in a circle.)

Then we pretend to orbit
until we get dizzy.

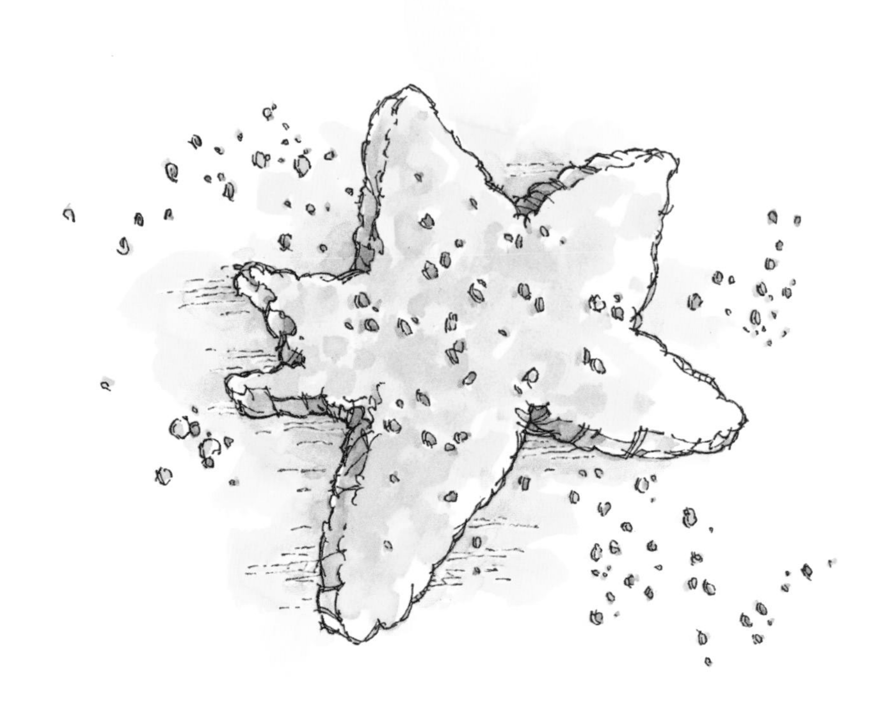

Later, we bake star cookies.

Sprinkles make them sparkle.

“The sun is a star,”

I tell my sister.

“It is the closest star,

so we see it in the day.”

After dinner,

we wait for the baby-sitter.

She is very late.

Dad says not to worry.

We have plenty of time.

At last we get in the car.

Drip, drip, drip.

It is raining.

The rain comes down
harder and harder.
Dad drives slower and slower.
It is getting later and later.

A policeman comes over.

"The road is closed,"

he tells my parents.

"There is too much water."

Oh no!

There are cars in front of us.

There are cars behind us.

We are stuck!

"The show is starting soon!"

Robert says.

"We will not make it."

Drip, drip, drip goes the rain.

Drip, drip, drip go my tears.

Robert and I are so sad.

We do not even want any cookies.

At last the cars move

and the rain stops.

But it is too late.

The night sky show is over.

By the time we get home,
the sky is full of stars.
They are brilliant!
(That's a fancy word
for shiny and bright.)

I get a brilliant idea.

(Brilliant also means very smart.)

We can have

our own night sky show.

My parents get my sister.

We set up beach chairs.

Mom lights candles.

Dad puts the cookies on a tray.

We eat alfresco.

(That's fancy for eating outdoors.)

We watch the stars.

We see the North Star.

We see the Big Dipper.

All at once,

something zooms across the sky.

“A shooting star,” Dad says.

“Make a wish!”

I tell Dad it is not a star.

It is a meteor.

But I make a wish anyway.

The next day Ms. Glass says,
“Everyone missed the show
because of the storm.
So we will go next week.”
Everybody is very happy.
And guess what? My wish came true!

Fancy Nancy's Fancy Words

These are the fancy words in this book:

Alfresco—outside; eating outside is called eating alfresco

Brilliant—bright and shiny, or very, very smart

Constellation—a group of stars that make a picture

Fascinating—very interesting

Meteor—a piece of a comet that leaves a blazing streak as it travels across the sky (you say it like this: me-tee-or)

Orbit—to circle around something

Planetarium—a museum about stars and planets